Fast Track

Anthony Hampshire

Fitzhenry & Whiteside

Published in Canada by Fitzhenry & Whiteside,
195 Allstate Parkway, Markham, Ontario L3R 4T8

Published in the United States by Fitzhenry & Whiteside,
311 Washington Street, Brighton, Massachusetts 02135

www.fitzhenry.ca   godwit@fitzhenry.ca

10 9 8 7 6 5 4 3 2 1

Fitzhenry & Whiteside acknowledges with thanks the Canada Council
for the Arts and the Ontario Arts Council for their support of our
publishing program. We acknowledge the financial support of
the Government of Canada through the Book Publishing Industry
Development Program (BPIDP) for our publishing activities.

Canada Council   Conseil des Arts
for the Arts   du Canada

ONTARIO ARTS COUNCIL
CONSEIL DES ARTS DE L'ONTARIO

Library and Archives Canada Cataloguing in Publication
Hampshire, Anthony, 1951-
Fast track / Anthony Hampshire.
(Redline racing series)
ISBN 1-55041-570-0
I. Title. II. Series.
PS8565.A5663F37 2005   jC813'.6   C2005-905223-6

U.S. Publisher Cataloging-in-Publication Data
(Library of Congress Standards)

Hampshire, Anthony, 1951-
Fast track / Anthony Hampshire.
[138] p. : cm. (Redline racing series)
Summary: Eddie and his friends sink their savings into
a Trans-Am Mustang and enter it into their first pro race; but
they soon learn that it takes more than skill to win a race,
as some drivers play by their own set of rules.
ISBN 1-55041-570-0 (pbk.)
1. Automobile racing — Juvenile literature — Fiction. I. Title. II. Series.
[Fic] —dc22   PZ7.H34Fa   2005

Design by Wycliffe Smith Design Inc.
Cover photo courtesy of Eric Gilbert, Motorsport.com

Printed in Canada

Fast Track

For Maureen, Ali, and Cait.
You were right!
—*A.H.*

Acknowledgements

I am very grateful to my editor Ann Featherstone, whose insight and thoroughness have greatly improved this story; and to Gail Winskill at Fitzhenry & Whiteside for her constant support and encouragement. I owe a special debt of gratitude to Justin Sofio, driver for the Mathiasen Motorsports/RLM Investments Formula Atlantic team in California, and to Cam Binder of Binder Racing in Calgary. Justin and Cam graciously adopted me as a crew member, patiently answered all of my technical questions about their Swift 008 race car, and even gave me an official team hat.

Chapter 1

Bad Idea

Rick had looked better. A lot better. He lay motionless on an examining table in the emergency room. The harsh overhead lights brought out every shade of gray and pale green on his drawn face. Behind the wire rimmed glasses, only his eyes offered some evidence of life.

The nurse checked his IV tube again, smiled bravely at us, and left, drawing the curtain behind her. In the early hours of the morning, the stillness of the ward was only disturbed by the soft hiss of the air conditioner. Rick looked up at me.

"Eddie...," he whispered faintly.

I bent lower. "Right here, buddy."

"Eddie, I just want you to know something important. Really important."

"Save it. Wait until you're stronger," I replied.

Slowly Rick drew himself up on one elbow, pain etching his face.

"No...it's got to be now. I've got to say it. Eddie, about what happened—"

"It's over," I replied. "Don't blame—"

"You!" He spat the word out between clenched teeth.

"You?" I responded blankly. "Don't blame you? No way I'm blaming my best—"

Rick reached up with his other hand, grabbed my collar, and pulled me to within inches of his face. "I mean you, Eddie. I blame you.... No one else, just...you."

Rick fell back onto the pillow, turning an even paler shade of gray than before. "It was your dumb idea."

He was right. During all the confusion of the past few hours, I hadn't really admitted it fully to myself yet. But the truth was that if I hadn't sparked Rick's fertile imagination in the first place, we would be sleeping peacefully in the cab of our truck under the Oregon stars instead of winding up here in the Yamhill County Emergency Room. I should have known. Rick Grant—mechanical engineer, software developer, race car designer, and my best friend since junior high—had one of those minds that finds a solution and puts it into action before most people have even begun to figure out what the question was. While I needed a minute or two to think things through, Rick had usually already made the next leap and was on to steps that no one else had thought of. He had been like that for as long as I'd known him.

From grade seven through twelve, Rick's warp-speed brain not only got him a wall full of science fair ribbons and scholarship certificates, it also landed him in hot water with his teachers—for constantly finishing their sentences for them. And sometimes, like this time, it launched him headlong into situations that backfired. I know that, and I should have seen it coming. I sat down in a cracked plastic chair, stared at the gray-streaked lino floor (curiously, almost exactly the same color as my best friend's face), and slowly shook my head.

"Evening, boys!"

A deep voice resonated behind me. I turned and saw the shiny, black leather boots first. Then, as my eyes traveled upward, I took in the navy blue wool pants with the red side stripe, the thick, black leather belt, a holstered pistol, a navy nylon jacket, and finally the embroidered shoulder crest of the Oregon State Highway Patrol. This couldn't be good. Slowly, I got to my feet.

"Good evening, Officer." I avoided making eye contact, trying to conceal my nervousness. "I was just sitting with my friend here," I offered.

"Yes, you were," the uniform replied. "I've been just outside the door for a few minutes, watching and listening. Quite a touching bedside scene," he stated, and smiled thinly.

"Didn't want to spoil the moment," he added, more with sarcasm than sympathy. "Especially the part where he told you it's your fault. That was especially good."

I could feel my hands beginning to sweat and the color draining from my face. Maybe I was starting to look like Rick. Maybe it was infectious. Maybe I was just in big trouble.

"Am I in big trouble?"

"Oh yes, I think so." He pulled out a leather notebook and opened it. "In fact, I think it's safe to say that you, your friend here, and the other guy—the really big guy outside with my partner—are all in it up to your ears. So, how about you just relax and let's see what we've got."

I sat quietly, waiting for the details I knew all too well but hoped that he didn't. The patrolman began.

"Let's start with names," he said, looking at me.

"Edward Stewart. Call me Eddie. Everyone does," I replied.

"All right, Eddie. And you?" he asked, looking over at Rick.

"Richard Grant, sir. Just Rick is fine."

Our names were carefully recorded in a black leather notebook.

"You know, boys, Thursday nights are generally pretty quiet around here. In fact, I can't remember the last time I had a high-speed pursuit. But then dispatch called in about 2:00 a.m. Seems old Mr. and Mrs. Collier, both of them deaf as posts, had been woken up by a Stealth jet fighter. That's exactly what they said it was, 'a Stealth jet fighter,' blasting past their house. No lights, just thundering noise, wind, and speed."

The patrolman flipped back a page in his notebook. "At 2:11 a.m., I turn onto Interstate 5 about three miles out of town, cruising at about sixty. Everything's peaceful, not a soul on the road…" He stopped, looked up, and smiled expectantly.

"And guess what happened then?" he asked.

I looked down at Rick. He hadn't moved, but he was definitely following every word of the conversation with growing alarm, his eyes darting back and forth between me and the patrolman.

"Just a second. Officer, I'm sorry, but I didn't get your name." It was a weak attempt to buy a few seconds, but I needed it to sort out what I was going to say.

"Collier. Officer Collier."

Perfect. Terrorize old folks at 2:00 a.m. Better yet, terrorize Officer Collier's folks. He had his pen and notebook ready and waiting.

"Now, Mr. Stewart—Eddie. What do you think happened then?" he repeated.

I looked at Rick again. He had pulled the sheet up, so only his eyes were exposed. He looked at me, nodded, and pulled the sheet the rest of the way over his head.

"And then...," I began slowly. "Then you were instantly passed by a race car. A Trans-Am Mustang, red, white, and black, number 75, with no lights, no plates, no windows..."

"Don't forget mufflers," Officer Collier added helpfully.

"Right. No mufflers," I admitted.

"Exactly! And this Mustang was a pretty good match for the Stealth jet fighter my dad saw. What a coincidence. So, about how fast would you say old number 75 was traveling, Eddie?"

"Well, it's hard to say, Officer. You see, there's no

speedometer in a race car. Just a tachometer that shows engine revs and—"

A muffled voice came uncertainly from under the bedsheet. It was Rick.

"Probably about 150 miles per hour.… Maybe a bit more, with the gears we've got in it for Monterey."

"Well, he's alive!" exclaimed Officer Collier in mock surprise. "Look, Eddie! It seems that Rick here has made a stunning recovery. And, even better, he seems to know a lot about Trans-Am Mustangs."

"Of course I do," Rick said, lowering the sheet and sitting up slowly. "I designed that car."

"And I drive it," I added. "I mean I drove it. And the three of us were all inside. Look, Officer, we're a race team on our way to the Champ Car race in Monterey, California, this weekend. There's a Trans-Am race as a preliminary, and we're entered."

While this sounded entirely sensible to me, it was clear from the notes Officer Collier was making that, for him, it was just the beginning of the most interesting Thursday night he'd had in years.

Chapter 2

The Man of Steel

Officer Collier looked up from his notepad.

"Monterey, California? Well, you know, I've been down there with my boys a few times to see the races. And I'd say that most—no, actually I'd say *all*—of the race teams I've ever seen have trailers and tow trucks. They don't drive their race cars on public roads to get to the track, now do they, boys?"

"No, they don't," I replied. "And we don't either. Honest. Except this time we just had to." I gestured gently toward the bed. "For Rick."

Removing his glasses, Rick looked up at us with his best "lost puppy" eyes.

"You know I chased you boys all the way to the hospital. Lights, siren on, pedal flat to the floor. I've got the big Police Interceptor motor but I couldn't catch you till you decided to make a little pit stop in the emergency department driveway. So, what's the deal? Appendicitis? Snake bite?"

"Gas," Rick said quietly.

"Gas?" Officer Collier was starting to enjoy this. He wrote GAS in big letters in the notebook and underlined it. Twice.

"Yes. We, uh…we had an urgent gas problem," I stated.

Officer Collier was struggling for control, biting his lower lip hard, trying not to laugh us all the way out of Emergency and into the county jail. I looked over at Rick, who seemed to be growing annoyed that his condition was not being taken seriously. He sat up and swung his legs out of bed and onto the floor. I caught the IV cart just in time.

"Excuse me, Officer," Rick said sternly, looking him straight in the eye. "But this was a serious situation. I am a professional engineer, and let me tell you that gas is no laughing matter. Gas is a complex substance. It is very hard to store. It is dangerously toxic. And the kind of gas we're talking about is highly explosive. My teammates are very careful around it."

"You bet we are," I added.

This was almost too much for Collier. Although he covered his mouth with his writing hand and kept his jaw clamped firmly shut, little tears were beginning to form at the corners of his eyes. He was clearly a man under great stress. He cleared his throat.

"Well, I can't argue with that, Rick. Gas can be a...very serious business. Goodness knows, even though they're special and I love 'em, if I have too many blazing saddle beans with my fajitas, well..." He grinned at us.

Rick was confused. "Beans? What do you mean, beans?"

Before we could hear more on this subject from Officer Collier, the curtain parted and the Emergency resident entered. She was in her late twenties, tall and very businesslike. She put Rick back into bed, covered him up, checked the IV, and made a note on his bedside chart. She looked up at Collier.

"Hello, Ben. Haven't seen you since Halloween," she said.

"Hi, Doc. Halloween's always weird, but, you know, I think this one might be even better. It seems these two are part of some race car team on their way to Monterey this weekend. And young Rick here had a major gas attack. Somehow that got them into their Mustang race car doing 160 down the interstate and in here. What did they tell you?" he asked the resident.

Slowly the resident's businesslike expression relaxed into a smile as she looked at Rick and me.

"Well, this young man was in a bad way when he arrived, but he did not have a gas problem. At least not the kind you might be thinking of. He did, however, have a serious emergency with gasoline. High-octane racing gasoline, I believe, which he had somehow managed to drink—"

Rick interrupted. "I swallowed it by accident. I didn't drink it."

Officer Collier was grinning again as he wrote furiously. Without looking up, he asked, "And how exactly did you come to swallow gasoline?"

Rick pulled the sheet over his head again and groaned. "Tell him, Eddie. And remember, it was your idea."

So I told him. I told him how we decided to take a midnight shortcut with our truck and trailer across some Oregon back roads, and got lost. How we drove around in circles for two hours, then ran out of gas. How I left my cellphone at the shop, and then came up with the idea to get some gas out of the Mustang, put it in the truck, and try to find the main highway again. How Rick was out the door in a flash, inside the trailer, and had a hose down the Mustang's fuel filler before we caught up to him. And how Rick had put the hose in his mouth to create suction and get the fuel flowing, but instead got a mouthful of gas, gagged, swallowed it, doubled over, and started turning gray. Then I told them about Herb. How he decided that we had to get Rick to a hospital immediately and the only way to do that was to unload the Mustang race car, fire it up, pile everyone in, find the highway, and look for a blue Hospital sign. Officer Collier was getting near the end of his notebook as he wrote it all down.

"That's what they told me when they arrived, Ben," the resident stated. "And we did pump a nasty amount of gasoline out of his stomach. Good thing they got him here as fast as they did."

"OK." Collier closed the notebook and slipped it into his jacket pocket. "I think I've got this now. You, Rick, and this Herb fellow were on a high-speed emergency run to the hospital in a race car at 2:00 a.m. I'm going to have to think about this one. I still don't get one thing, though," he said.

"What's that?" I asked.

"Well, why did you need a hose to siphon gas out of the tank? Why not just turn on the ignition in that Mustang, undo a fuel line, and pump some out?" Collier asked.

I looked blankly at Rick. Collier was right. It was so

obvious. We hadn't thought things through. We had panicked. We were idiots.

"Didn't think of that, did you? All right, where's the Mustang now?" he asked.

"We left it around back," I replied. "Where's Herb?"

Collier zipped up his jacket. "He's out in the lobby with my partner. Truck keys, please." I gave them to him. "The Mustang stays put, and so do you three until I sort this out. Let's give Rick here a chance to rest, and go find Herb."

We opened the curtain, walked down the hallway, and rounded the corner into the waiting area. It was deserted except for a second patrolman and a nurse, who was on her phone at the admitting desk. There was no sign of Herb. That was strange because I'd left him in the waiting area, and guys Herb's size are hard to miss. Then we noticed a pile of candy bars, chip bags, and packages of mints under a bank of chairs. We walked up, peered over the chair backs, and found Herb, flat on his back, wrestling with a large chrome vending machine.

He had the machine on its side with the front panel off, its entire contents spread out on the waiting room floor. He was slowly bending two of the large metal vending containers into shape. I had seen Herb do this to machines before. Toasters, lawn mowers, mountain bikes, TV sets. It didn't matter. There was nothing Herb hated more than a machine, any machine, that wouldn't work properly, and he believed that he had been put on this earth to fix them. And he always did—with his bare hands, if necessary.

Rick and I had met Herb at a summer camp when we were all in junior high school. We called him the Man of Steel, not only because of his awesome strength but mostly because he looked exactly like Superman's human double, Clark Kent. He had jet black hair with that little curl at the front, the heavy black framed glasses, and at 6 feet, 4 inches and 240 pounds of solid muscle, you could almost see him exiting a phone booth and leaping tall buildings with a single bound, cape and all.

Herb looked up from the floor at Collier and me. The Man of Steel spoke.

"Hi guys. Just about done. I'll button this thing back up and be right with you."

Herb replaced the vending trays, the candy, chips, and mints, hung the door back on its hinges, stood the machine upright, and plugged it in. He put in some change, and pushed the button for some barbecue chips. The machine hummed quietly, and a bag of chips was released effortlessly into Herb's waiting hand. He smiled the Clark Kent smile. Herb's work here was done. Satisfied, he turned to face us.

"It's good now," Herb said as he opened the bag. "The nurse said this machine hadn't worked for weeks. Just needed some adjustment. They all do. Chip?"

We both shook our heads.

"So, how's Rick?"

"He's had his stomach pumped and he's resting now." I replied. "The doctor says he'll be a lot better by morning. Herb, this is Officer Collier of the Oregon Highway Patrol."

Herb wiped his hand on his jeans and extended it. Collier accepted, realizing too late that shaking hands with Herb was exactly like putting your fingers in a vise. Herb smiled as Collier winced in pain.

"Herb MacDonald. Glad to meet you, Officer. I'm the crew chief on our Trans-Am car. We're on our way to Monterey to race this weekend and—"

Collier, trying to rub some life back into his hand, cut him short.

"Yes, I know all that. Look, I want you two to stay here with your friend. I'm going to run this whole deal past my boss. I could lock you guys up, write a list of violations a foot long, and impound the Mustang and your truck, wherever it is, right now.

But I won't. At least, not yet. It's one thing to pile three guys into a race car with one seat, no lights, and no mufflers, and use public highways as your own personal racetrack. It's another thing to respond to an emergency situation."

"So you aren't charging us?" I asked hopefully.

Collier spoke carefully. "Don't know. I might yet. But it's not clear to me that you had any other option than using that Mustang to save your friend. You thought his life was in danger, you had to act fast, and you used what you had to save him. Sounds like everyone lost their heads. So in this case there appear to be, as we say, 'extenuating circumstances.' And you three have been up front with me. I appreciate honesty, however strange it may sound. So, stay put. I'll be back soon."

Collier left his partner to keep an eye on us, got back in his patrol car, and went to wake up his boss. Herb leaned over to me and whispered, "Extenuating circumstances? Think that's good?"

"Maybe," I replied. "If they see it as an emergency, we might not get charged." I was dog tired. "Let's get some rest."

Herb and I took a couch each in the waiting room and tried to get some sleep. Siphoning the gas had been a really dumb idea. We could easily have pumped the gas out using the Mustang's own fuel pumps. Then fixing that mistake had landed us in a bigger mess. But it looked like Rick was recovering fast, and Officer Collier was willing to cut us a break. Maybe he just felt sorry for us. I would have, in his place.

Through the window, the first rays of dawn started to turn the clouds light pink and orange. We were supposed to be at Laguna Seca Raceway in Monterey, California, in five hours. We were going to be late.

Chapter 3

On the Road

I woke up a couple of hours later, after dreaming that Herb and I had been lost at sea in a brightly colored rubber raft, after our vending machine had been torpedoed and sunk by the highway patrol. Weird. I guess that came from last night's panic, lack of sleep, and the orange vinyl couch that I had slept on. I noticed that my cheek seemed to have bonded with the cushion. I checked my watch, slowly peeled my face off the couch, got up, and shuffled over to Herb. He had the yellow couch.

"Herb. Wake up. It's after seven," I droned. Nothing.

"Herb! Come on! Rise and shine!" I shouted, clapping my hands.

Not even a twitch. This did not surprise me. Among the many talents of the Man of Steel was his ability to sleep through any known wake-up call, train wrecks, and most natural disasters. I have seen Herb sleep for hours next to a nine-drawer tool chest in the back of a van careening down a mountain forestry road. I have seen him nod off inside his truck as it goes through the automatic car wash. I have personally tried to wake him up in his apartment by letting the phone ring for ten minutes, and then banging on his door until all his neighbors came into the hall. So this was nothing new. The summer I met Herb at camp, four of us discovered that the only effective method to get him up was to carry him each morning, still in his cot, down to the swimming pool, and place him on the end of the diving board. Then we would wait for him to turn over and roll off into the pool. Sometimes we waited half an hour. But it was always worth it.

Herb can work day and night if he's got something to fix or make, but once he's asleep, forget trying to wake him up. So I left him snoring on the yellow couch and went past the admissions desk and up the hall to see how Rick was doing. There was no sign of Officer Collier's partner. I pulled back the curtain and found the bed made and Rick showered, dressed, and ready to go. The gray and green skin tones were gone, and he looked human again.

"Eddie! Good to see you. Man, what a night!" he chirped.

I was surprised. "You look good, Rick. Feel OK?"

He grinned. "Excellent. Slept like a baby. Maybe I should drink gas more often."

"Has the doctor seen you yet?" I asked

"She just left. Says I'm fine to leave. So, come on, let's get going. We need to get to Monterey and set up the car," Rick said, full of energy and purpose.

"Hold on. Did you forget about last night?" I reminded him. "The lost truck? An emergency run in the Mustang? Officer Collier?"

Rick sat down heavily on the bed. "Yeah, right. What did he say?"

"He left about four this morning to talk with his boss—the police chief, I guess. I think he was going to put in a good word for us. I think he understands that it was an emergency," I explained.

"Then we won't be going to jail?" Rick said.

I pulled back the curtain. "Don't know yet. Officer Collier left his partner here last night. Let's see if we can find him and see what's going on."

Rick and I walked back to the lobby, past a snoring Herb, and found the cafeteria. I spotted Collier's partner in the corner having breakfast with Rick's doctor, the emergency resident. We walked over.

"Good morning, gentlemen," the doctor said brightly. "Still feeling all right?" she asked Rick.

"Fine. Thanks to you. I really appreciate your help,"

he replied.

"Well, you're free to go, Rick," she said, rising from the table. "At least as far as the medical profession is concerned." She smiled at Collier's partner, picked up her tray, and left.

The patrolman motioned for us to sit. We did, waiting for the verdict. He took a sip of coffee from his cup and savored it.

"Best coffee in town. And in the hospital, of all places."

He read the anxiety in our faces. "Officer Collier called about an hour ago. You're clear to go. "

"Great!" Rick yelled.

I wanted to be sure. "So, you're letting us off? No charges?"

He nodded. "No charges. Collier and the chief both saw it as an emergency situation. Actually, they thought it too weird not to be true. And pretty funny. This is one for the next squad meeting. Anyway, no more race cars on public roads."

We quickly agreed.

"We also found your truck and trailer about ten miles north. There's a gas station a few blocks from here, and I had them take some gas out for the truck and drive it back here. The rig's parked out back, next to that Mustang of yours."

I was amazed. "I can't believe this. We wake up half the county, lead you guys on a high-speed chase, and take up your whole night. And now you're helping us on our way?"

The patrolman finished his coffee, got up from his chair, and began to put on his jacket.

"All part of the job." He stopped and smiled. "Actually, last night was the best entertainment we've had in months. Just think of this as our way of showing our appreciation. And guys, Officer Collier recommended that you get yourselves a cellphone. For the next time, OK? Have a safe trip."

"Unbelievable," Rick muttered as we watched the patrolman leave the cafeteria.

"Just be thankful some people still have a good sense of humor," I said. I got up from the table.

"All right. Let's get Sleeping Beauty and hit the road."

It took both of us, but we managed to get Herb upright and on his feet, then half drag him to the truck, where we folded him into the back seat of the crew cab. He did not wake up. We pushed the Mustang back inside the trailer, pulled out of the hospital, filled up at the station, and got on the interstate for Laguna Seca Raceway, Monterey, California.

Chapter 4

Laguna Seca

The 400 miles to the Pacific coast town of Monterey passed quickly, but as I had feared, we arrived in the late afternoon, well after all the other teams had set up their pits and completed both practice sessions. We put our car through the required technical inspection, and were assigned the only pit that was left, at the end of the paved paddock area. In the gravel. We set up our pit equipment, began unloading our spare tires, tools, and work tables, and put up an awning to provide some shade. Herb had finally woken up, and he began to unload his tool chests. Nobody touched Herb's tool chests except him. That's because no one else could lift them. It took us an hour to set everything up, and then Rick sat us down for a meeting.

"OK, race fans. We've missed practice completely.

So we have no baseline data to help us set the car up for qualifying tomorrow morning. Any ideas?" he asked.

"We should eat," Herb stated.

"Eat?" Rick replied as he powered up his laptop computer. "Herb, we're going to have to find a setup for qualifying. We have to change springs, change gears, and do a full chassis alignment tonight."

"I know," Herb said calmly. "That's why we need to eat first. So we'll be alert. So we won't make any dumb mistakes. Like inhale gas."

I stepped in before Rick could take up the challenge.

"Herb's right. I'll unhook the trailer, take the truck, and get some food. You guys want the usual?"

They nodded and I left. Driving out of the track, I began to feel comfortable again. We had survived a near disaster, we had finally arrived at one of the great racetracks in America, and now we were getting ready to compete tomorrow as professionals. I didn't mind being the "gofer" (go fer this, go fer that). That was part of my job. Rick and Herb built the car, prepared it, and argued. I rarely did much of the real work on it. It was clear to them that my main job was to drive it, and to keep them fed.

Driving the short distance into Monterey, it

occurred to me how great it was that the three of us were here at all, doing what we had always wanted to, and what we had worked hard to become good at. We had known each other for almost ten years, and began racing together three years ago. Rick and I grew up on the same shady street in Vancouver, British Columbia, and Herb was from Seattle, Washington. The three of us became fast friends at a junior high youth summer camp on Vancouver Island. We kept in touch by mail, and got together in the summers at Rick's parents' cottage on the Oregon coast.

The year I started grade eight, my mom died. Cancer. It was a tough summer for Dad and me, and the only things that made it bearable for me were my Aunt Sophie and weekends with the guys at Portland International Raceway, where we watched anything with wheels race. When we finished high school, Herb went to work in his dad's machine shop, and Rick went to Caltech, in Los Angeles, on an engineering scholarship. I stayed home and studied communications at the University of British Columbia by day, and spent my nights waiting on tables in my Aunt Sophie's Italian restaurant.

A few years later, we decided to try our hand at racing, and it only seemed sensible that Rick and Herb would look after the car and that I would drive it and look after the food. While it quickly became clear to Aunt Sophie and my dad that I didn't have a bright future in the restaurant business, I did want to be a professional racing driver some day. From my first ten minutes behind the wheel of a racing car at the Jim Russell Racing School in California—a high-school graduation gift from Aunt Sophie—I knew that I wanted to do nothing else. And the best part was that I was good at it, graduating at the top of the rookie class and winning the school's summer Formula Ford Series. Herb was there to lend a hand, and Rick loved the cars, even taking the school himself before he crashed. Rick didn't talk about that.

That summer, we learned that it was definitely much more fun to race ourselves than to watch other people do it. I found out that I could wheel a race car, Rick immediately understood the physics and engineering side, and Herb could make, fix, or modify anything. Together, we had the ingredients for a strong race team, and by Christmas we had decided to go ahead and get a car. We pooled all the money we had, topped that up with loans from Rick's parents and my dad, and bought a slightly used Van Dieman Formula Ford. Herb's dad gave us the back of his machine shop in Seattle for a base, and Rick and I drove there every other weekend during the winter months to prepare the car.

That summer, we raced in amateur races all over the Pacific Northwest and California. Confident that Rick had given me the best-engineered car on the grid and that Herb had made it as reliable as an anvil, I drove the wheels off that Van Dieman and we won the PacWest Formula Ford Championship. The following spring, Rick and I graduated from college. By then, Herb's reputation as an ace machinist was growing and he had opened a second shop with his dad.

I recalled a particular Sunday afternoon barbecue that our parents organized for us, where they sat us all down to talk about "the future." I knew that they were concerned with their boys playing high-risk sports like car racing. It was one of those serious parent-to-young-man conversations about career planning, goal setting, and making sensible decisions for the future. Rick's dad, the stock market analyst, talked about growth industries, solid professions, and emerging markets. They asked us what our plans were. We told them we wanted to keep on racing— not only in amateur events, but to eventually work our way up to a level where we could one day make a living at it as professionals.

They talked to us about the risks. And especially

about the money. I remember my dad, the accountant, asking us how to make a million dollars in racing. We didn't know. He told us that you start with two million.

These memories came back vividly as I pulled into BurgerWorld ("A Planet of Patties!") and parked the truck. And I had to smile at the way our parents had eventually come around. Once they saw that we were serious and that we had a plan, they came onside. The three of us agreed to put everything we had into making it as professionals within three years, and our folks offered us their support as well. That same spring we sold the Formula Ford, deciding that the next step closer to the professional ranks was to get into a faster car. Our ultimate goal was to work our way up the ladder to an open-wheeled 800-horsepower Champ Car, but lacking a spare eight million dollars to do that, we looked at trying to get into the faster Formula cars, like Formula Atlantic. We did the math and found that we were still a long way from making the step to that level. But we could afford, just, to build and run a car for the Sports Car Club of America (SCCA) Trans-Am championship, a pro series for heavily modified road cars like Mustangs, Corvettes, and Camaros.

Although I wanted to stay with single-seat, open-wheel Formula cars, the budget just wasn't there.

But, if we built it ourselves, we could afford a decent Trans-Am car, get some pro experience in a much faster series, make some prize money, and maybe attract some sponsors. So we all moved to Seattle that spring, built the Mustang in six weeks, and won the Northwest Amateur GT1 title with it that summer. And all of that had brought us here to Laguna Seca, preparing for our first professional race. And the delights of BurgerWorld.

Chapter 5

Fast Eddie

I got back to our pit with the usual. Three loaded triple burgers, jumbo bags of fries, and three milkshakes. That was for Herb. Rick and I found that one of everything was ample. They had the Mustang raised up on steel stands, and, stripped of its wheels and body panels, it was a cage made up of a mass of steel tubes. Herb was working under the car.

"Supper ready yet?" Herb asked.

"Patience," I replied. "Great food takes time to prepare."

"So you should be ready in the next twenty seconds, right?"

I unpacked supper and laid it out on a folding metal work bench. Rick was busy working on his laptop, running calculations for the gearing and suspension settings he thought we would need. I peered over his shoulder.

"Any ideas?" I asked.

Rick removed his glasses and rubbed his eyes. "It's a guess, but I think we'll be in the ballpark. Herb's making the changes now. The good news is that you've raced here before."

That was true, and might be an advantage for us. I had completed the Jim Russell Racing School at Laguna Seca and we had raced there twice with the Formula Ford. Still, a 600-horsepower Trans-Am car on this track was a whole different beast. Winning the GT1 regional title took a fast car, and we knew we had one. But we had never run up against professionals with big-dollar budgets. This was a different game. None of the teams at Laguna Seca that weekend were racing for fun, for honor, or for a trophy. It was business, not pleasure. They were there to win.

I left Rick to his laptop and walked back

to the trailer to grab some cans of soda. I paused and said over my shoulder, "Just set it up on the easy side until I see how it feels. If it's really a dog, I'll come in during qualifying, but let's just make sure I can get it on the grid."

Rick didn't look up from his keyboard.

"No sweat. You'll be Fast Eddie tomorrow," Rick stated confidently. "Count on it."

Saturday morning dawned clear and hot, with a piercing blue sky. Herb and Rick had sent me to bed early while they worked well past midnight getting the car ready. We usually got motel rooms, but with our delay in Oregon, we couldn't afford to waste time traveling back and forth to the track. When needed, we could convert our thirty-five-foot aluminum trailer into a mobile workshop, including sleeping quarters and even a small kitchen. So we all slept, quite comfortably, inside the trailer.

Herb, who now had something mechanical to look after, was up at dawn and had made a pot of his famous triple-strength coffee. He called it "real coffee." We called it road tar. Herb firmly believed that if you were making coffee, or anything else for that matter, then it was to be done seriously. No fooling around. The distinctive aroma of this special brew woke me up. I got out of my sleeping bag, left the trailer, and poured myself a cup. As usual, it was a real jolt.

The Mustang was fully assembled again, its scarlet bodywork in place, crouched on its four massive slicks. I walked around to the rear of the car. Herb had squeezed himself inside, coffee in hand. He was talking softly. I went a few steps closer, and heard him speaking in a patient and serious tone. It was time for final instructions.

"Don't be nervous," he said slowly and quietly to the Mustang. "I know it's our first pro race, but we're ready. Rick and I have put you together exactly right. So go out there today and play nice. And don't hurt Eddie."

Then he bowed his head and was quiet.

Herb didn't know I was behind him. For a moment I thought about surprising him, but then I quietly walked back to the trailer. This was an important time for the Man of Steel. I'd seen him do this before, when he was putting together parts or assembling complete engines in the machine shop. To most people, racing cars were simply cold pieces of machinery. Not to Herb. He built them, cared for them, and talked to them. They were his pets.

Rick was up and moving around, looking for his

glasses.

"Herb made real coffee. Want some?" I asked.

"No way. I've done enough damage to my stomach already." Rick found his glasses, cleaned them, and put them on. "How about you get breakfast organized, and Herb and I will fuel and warm up the Mustang."

"Give him a minute," I said. Rick smiled to himself as I went into the mini-kitchen and began to mix up the ingredients for Herb's favorite meal, pancakes.

Breakfast was quickly out of the way, the car was warmed up, and I had changed into the worst possible clothing for a hot summer day in California—my driving suit. My outfit included long underwear, a turtleneck top, thick socks, and lightweight driving shoes topped off with a dark blue, quilted, triple-layer driving suit. All of it was fireproof. The idea was to offer fire protection for about a minute if you were ever caught inside a burning car, every driver's worst nightmare. I was thankful that I'd had never had to test it.

The track announcer gave the first call for Trans-Am qualifying. I stepped through the driver's window and slid down into the form-fitting racing seat, surrounded by the tubes and braces of the Mustang's frame and roll cage. I strapped myself firmly into the seat with the six-point safety harness, pulling it tight, so only my arms, legs, and head could move freely. Strapped into the car, I then squeezed in earplugs, pulled on a hood and my helmet, and finished with a pair of thick, blue driving gloves. All flameproof, of course. About the only things left exposed to the open air were my eyes.

Just sitting there, I was already uncomfortably warm. I knew that once I was out on the track, the heat from the engine and the physical exertion of driving would make things really hot.

The final item was the window safety net, which prevented a driver's arm from being flung out and crushed in the event of a wreck. Before fastening it, Rick leaned in.

"You're carrying twenty gallons, which should be enough to qualify with. We've only got thirty minutes to set a time. You've got fresh brake pads and a new set of tires, so go easy the first couple of laps. Watch your mirrors. There are a lot of fast cars here." Then he added with a wink, "And you're one of them."

I gave Rick the thumbs-up sign, switched on the ignition and the dual fuel pumps, and then pressed the starter button. The Mustang coughed once, then exploded into life, the racket from its big V-8 engine and open exhausts completely filling and vibrating everything inside the car. I checked the gauges to make sure that the oil pressure, water temperature, and fuel pressure were OK, made a slight adjustment to my rearview mirror, and nodded to Herb. He pushed the car out from under the trailer awning. I pushed in the clutch, selected first gear, and chugged slowly down the pit lane to join the qualifying lineup.

Two cars were rolling along in front of me. The three of us were waved right through into the pit lane, where we began accelerating to enter the track. Perfect. I hate lineups. I took things easy for the first three laps, refreshing my memory of Laguna Seca's eleven turns and giving the tires, brakes, and everything else lots of time to warm up properly before I put my foot down.

As I entered the main straight to begin my fourth lap, I had a quick glance at the gauges to make sure the engine was happy, checked for traffic in my mirrors, and decided it was time to unleash the Mustang. I gave it full throttle, lifting only for the split second it took to snap a shift up to the next gear from first to fifth. All of the 600 horses Herb had built into the engine were straining hard as the revs peaked at the end of the straight. Things were happening a lot more quickly now. The grandstands, fences, and guardrails became a blur, and the track rushed up at the windshield like a tidal wave. Cornering and braking forces tripled, pushing me hard into the seat and against the harness. Above it all, even with earplugs and a helmet, was the thundering blast of the Mustang's V-8.

With its variety of turns and hills, Laguna Seca is a great ride in a fast car, and I immediately felt that we had one. Rick had calculated suspension settings that made the Mustang handle like an ox cart at low speeds, but it improved greatly as the speed went up. In most road cars, the faster you go, the less control you have. But race cars, if they're set up well, actually handle better and become more rewarding to drive as speed increases. That was happening now with the Mustang as I completed four more laps, gradually going faster each time. The car braked straight and true, turned into corners immediately, and put the power down smoothly.

I was driving the course well except for the Corkscrew. This is a combination of corners at the top of a hill, and is the most challenging section on the course—maybe one of the toughest series of corners in American road racing. It demands hard braking from about 150 miles per hour, dropping down to second gear, and setting up to turn hard left as the road falls away steeply. You feel like you've been dropped off the roof of a tall building, then suddenly the road rushes back and snaps hard right, launching you out onto the back straight. Driving the Corkscrew well takes about two seconds, throws you hard left, hard right, drops you three stories, and launches you out onto the straight. Do it right and it's the best monster roller-coaster ride in road racing. Do it wrong and it will pitch you into, or over, the steel guardrails in a heartbeat.

I was driving the Corkscrew adequately but slowly, and I was losing time. I knew that I'd have to be both faster and, above all, smoother through there in the race. Otherwise, I was impressed with the car, and as I'd passed half a dozen other cars and no one had caught me, I was fairly confident that we must be setting some decent times. All too soon, the checkered flag was waved from the starter's tower, and the session was over. I backed off slowly; checking my gauges again on the cool-down lap, then came into the pits, coasted to a stop next to our trailer, and killed the engine. After the fury of qualifying, the sudden quiet inside the car seemed unreal.

I unbuckled the harness and window net, and climbed out the Mustang. My hair was soaked and matted to my head, and my driving suit felt like a wet sponge. Oddly, Herb and Rick were nowhere to be seen. Usually, they were waiting in our pit when

I came in. I went inside the trailer, closed the door, and gratefully began peeling off the layers of my driving suit. I heard Herb and Rick arrive back at the pit, and as soon as I'd changed into shorts and a T-shirt, I joined them. Rick had timed every lap of qualifying and was going over his notes with Herb. They weren't smiling.

"Sorry we're late," Rick said evenly. "We had to check something."

"So?" I asked anxiously. Rick and Herb looked solemnly at each other, then at me.

"Well…," Rick began slowly. "The stopwatch doesn't lie." Herb nodded and sighed.

"No way," I replied quickly. "I know I turned some fast laps out there. The car felt great. I must have passed five or six guys, and never saw anyone coming up on me the whole session. So, what's with the long faces?"

Then they caved in, grins spreading across their faces. "Seventh!" they announced together.

Rick was pumped. "Seventh! Twenty-four cars and we qualify seventh for our first Trans-Am!"

I grabbed the clipboard and read the time sheets carefully. "You're right! I mean, I thought we did OK, but seventh of twenty-four? Man, we're only a second and a bit off the pole winner's time."

Herb couldn't stop grinning.

"It's right. We checked with the official timers on our way back here. That's why we were late. All right, then," Herb said, with new purpose. "We race in three hours. First, I'll make some more coffee. Then, to work. So, Eddie, what does it need for the race? What do you want changed?"

"Nothing major," I replied, looking up from the time sheets. "I've got lots of power and the gearing is right. The rear shocks could maybe be a touch softer. And I'd like a bit more front brake. Other than that, leave it. It feels strong."

"OK, no sweat," said Rick. Then he added, "Speaking of sweat, you better air out that driving suit or use your spare. If you leave it piled up in the trailer, it might eat a hole in the floor."

I aired out the suit by stringing a makeshift clothesline between the truck and the trailer; although, after thinking about it, I decided to use my spare suit for the race. I wanted to start dry and comfortable. The scheduled race length was thirty laps, and as I squinted up at the sun, I knew it was going to be seriously hot when we took the green flag.

Chapter 6

Show Time

Herb and Rick had again put the Mustang back up on stands, stripped its bodywork, and were making the adjustments to the braking system and suspension that I had suggested. There wasn't much for me to do except watch and wait, and get nervous thinking about the race. Some drivers spend hours thinking through their every move before a race, but all that ever did for me was to give me a lot more to worry about. I always seemed to drive better when I got away from the pit for a while, took a walk, and tried to empty my mind. Once the race started for real, there would lots happening all at once. Better to be fresh mentally and physically. Which was why I decided that it was a good time to stroll the pits, find the driver's locker area, and grab a quick shower.

From where we were out in the gravel pit it was a long walk, but it was a good opportunity to check out the competition at work. Some of the teams looked like they were building new cars from scratch, frantically changing engines, transmissions, and complete rear ends. Some were making the same sort of fine adjustments that we were. And one team was slowly packing up to go home early, their Camaro bent and twisted beyond repair.

As I got nearer the main control tower, I came upon a large black transporter with three red Mustangs parked beside it. They were numbers 3, 5, and 9, all owned by a wealthy Ford dealer from Los Angeles, and I remembered from the time sheets Rick had shown me that the number 3 and 5 cars were both on the front row as the fastest qualifiers. I stopped and watched them for a few moments. The crewmen, all in matching, well-tailored uniforms, weren't doing much beyond checking tire pressures, fueling the cars, and waxing them. No major work or changes were underway. The three drivers sat in lawn chairs, sipping lemonade under a white canopy and sharing a joke. There was no panic here, just certainty. These guys were ready.

The next section of the pits was reserved for the open-wheeled Formula cars that would be racing tomorrow. On Sunday there would be a Formula Atlantic race, and then the main event for the Champ Cars late in the afternoon. Most of the Champ Cars were locked away in their trailers or transporters; but the Atlantic teams were qualifying soon, and they were busily preparing for the session. Like the Trans-Am field, there were all sorts of cars ranging from a couple of tired and dirty lumps of scrap held together with duct tape and wire—which I wouldn't have even sat in—to gleaming new Swifts, fresh from the factory. Much as I respected and appreciated our Mustang, the winged Atlantic cars with their shrieking twin-cam engines drew me like a magnet.

The last pit before the control tower is the best location, and it was occupied by a huge transporter with four bright yellow Formula Atlantic Swifts beside it.

All sat on a fresh green carpet and were being attended-ed to by a dozen mechanics, but with only two drivers. Then I realized that each driver had his race car as well as a spare. Not a spare engine, gearbox, or spare sets of wheels, like we had; these guys had two complete spare cars. Enjoying a catered lunch at tables with real linen tablecloths were a group of people who all looked like movie stars fresh from their yachts on the French Riviera. This outfit had big money written all over it. The transporter was pure gleaming white except for the legend "Ascension Motorsports, Sao Paulo, Brazil," printed in small black letters on its flank. Whoever they were, dollars were obviously not a problem.

The spectacle had attracted quite a crowd. I wanted to get a better look at the cars, so I stepped closer, only to be stopped by a chrome steel chain they had used to fence off their pit area and keep out the unwanted. You could only look into this world from a distance, and those on the inside seemed to enjoy the separation. Unlike other sports, how well you did in racing often came down to how good your equipment was rather than simply how good you were. And that usually meant how thick your wallet was. These guys looked like they would be pretty quick. No need for sponsors to pay the bills.

I carried on to the control tower and showered. Refreshed, I retraced my route back to our pit, secure in the knowledge that we wouldn't have to put up barriers anytime soon to keep the crowds out of our pit.

The Atlantic cars were out qualifying by this time, and I caught quick glimpses of them as they flashed past the pit area. One day, I thought, one day we'll be out there running with them.

As I entered our pit, I noticed that Herb had put a fresh set of slicks on the Mustang and was finishing filling the fuel tank with the forty gallons I would need to complete the race length of thirty laps. Gas mileage was not the Mustang's best feature. Rick looked up from checking tire pressures.

"Time to suit up, Eddie. These guys will be done their session in ten minutes." He stood and grinned. "And then, it's show time!"

The adrenaline was starting to flow for the three of us. I knew that every minute now would seem to drag on, as if in slow motion. While I suited up and got into the car, Rick and Herb loaded up a large pit cart with the tools, parts, and spare wheels that they might need if I had to come in during the race. At only thirty laps race distance, I didn't plan on having to make a pit stop; but they would be ready just in case.

Herb leaned in with some last minute instructions.

"Just play yourself in slowly. You don't need to win it on the first lap."

I nodded, started the Mustang, and drove slowly out of our pit and down to the grid to take up my number seven position on the fourth row. The two red Los Angeles Mustangs that I had admired earlier were on the front row as fastest qualifiers, followed by four Camaros of varying design—one of them next to me. Behind us, the rest of the field of twenty-four cars stretched back, side by side, to row twelve. I shut down the engine and waited as the rest of the cars took their places. Time dragged like molasses in January. Waiting for it to begin was always the worst part of any race. You're hot, you can't really move around, and there's not much to look at and no one to talk to. You're just stuck, listening to your heartbeat increase and trying to stay calm.

Finally, the Porsche pace car came out, and the starter rotated his green flag in the air, signaling us to start engines and roll out for the pace lap. I switched everything on, pressed the starter button, and felt the Mustang's engine instantly burst to life, along with twenty-four others. I waited while the two Camaros in front of me started to move, then grabbed first gear and got underway. As we picked up some speed, I shifted into second and began weaving the Mustang from side to side to warm the tires. I lifted off and braked early for the first left-hand turn, squeezing the brakes gently to allow the pads to warm. The pace car kept our speed down to about seventy miles per hour all the way around for two pace laps, and then pulled off before the final corner. I was seconds away from my first start as a professional.

Chapter 7

Rookie Mistake

The number 3 and 5 white Mustangs led the field out onto the main straight, and our speed began to build. I shifted up to third, with one eye on the Camaro right in front of me and the other on the starter's stand, watching for the drop of the flag to start the race. The starter seemed to be taking forever, but just as the front row almost went past him, he waved the green flag. Twenty-four right feet instantly went down hard, unleashing 12,000 horsepower in a furious explosion of noise. I wound the Mustang up to the limit in every gear, as a wall of raw power pushed me into the seat. I was right with the Camaros. We thundered over a slight crest near the end of the straight, lifted slightly for turn one, and began the short descent leading down to turn two, jumping hard on the brakes to slow from 150 to 40 miles per hour. I braked a fraction later than the Camaro on my left, and sliced in front of him as we entered the corner. Sixth place.

I downshifted to second for the tight left-hand hairpin, turned the Mustang in smoothly, and then got on the power early, hanging the tail out a bit as I accelerated hard and snapped a shift into third.

I pulled alongside the fifth-place Camaro. Turn three came up at us fast, and I had to ease off slightly, tuck in behind him through the middle of the turn, and then accelerate up to fourth and then fifth gear along the short straight leading into turn four. I was inches off his back bumper as I lifted for a heartbeat through the fast right-hander, then got hard on the gas again for turn five, a quick left, which led us onto the uphill portion of the course.

Turns six and seven were fast, sweeping left-hand corners, leading to the top part of the course. The uphill section has two rises, and we were side by side flat out in fifth over both of them. At the top of the hill, I had the inside line as we braked hard for the Corkscrew, and I reminded myself to be smooth. I made sure that I left my braking late enough to prevent the Camaro from darting in front of me at the downhill left-hand entrance to the Corkscrew. He had no option but to lift off and follow me through, as the road dropped steeply left, then right. I exited the

Corkscrew with the Mustang pulling hard and the Camaro in my mirrors. Fifth place.

I accelerated quickly on the downhill back straight, flat out through a slight left-hand kink, lifted briefly through turn ten, then back hard on the throttle to set up for the final corner. Turn eleven is a sharp second gear left-hander requiring hard and precise braking. It is also the single best place at Laguna Seca to pass someone. The Camaro I had just put down a place decided he wanted it back, and he came up quickly underneath me on the left. Too quickly. We both realized in the same instant that he was carrying too much speed to make the corner. I stood on the brakes, briefly locking my front tires, as he shot across my nose, went sideways across the track and backed into the guardrail on the outside of the corner. I unlocked my brakes, turned in and made the corner. Fourth place.

Taking up the Mustang to full speed on the straight, I had a moment to check my mirrors and glance at my gauges. Everything looked good under the hood, and there were no immediate threats from behind. I was in fourth about two seconds back of the leaders. Quite a first lap. I set my sights on catching the lead group, and knew that I could do it a fraction of a second every lap using Rick's chassis setup to make up time in the corners, and under-braking.

As the laps mounted, I used my knowledge of the track to get into a rhythm with the car, making all of my motions as smooth as possible, and allowing the Mustang to find its cornering and braking limits. I was also getting updates from Herb every time I passed the pits. We couldn't afford a radio setup, so he held up a pit board, which told me how many laps were complete, my position, and, most importantly, how far ahead the next car was. In the next eleven laps, I narrowed the gap to the leading group from four seconds to just under one.

The Mustang turned onto the main straight and then put its power down without a twitch as I took it up through the gears, building speed for the start/finish line and the beginning of lap thirteen. I was now close enough to mount an attack for third place. I checked Herb's pit board as I flashed past, saw the gap was reduced to half a second, and focused all my attention on catching and outbraking the Camaro that was now right in front of me by the end of the straight. Just as I came over the rise before turn one, I was stunned to see, out of the corner of my eye, a white Corvette inching up on my inside. Where had he come from? Then I realized I had been so focused on closing the gap to the leaders for the last few laps that I had forgotten to check what was happening behind me. That was what mirrors were for. It was a rookie mistake, and I knew it was going to cost me fourth place.

As things turned out, it cost me a lot more than that. The Corvette had the inside line for turn one, but I was determined that he was going to have to outdrive me to keep it. I left my braking to the last possible moment, and eased the Mustang into the corner, right on the limit. I had successfully outbraked the Corvette but left him no place to go except into the side of my car. He tapped me, surprisingly gently, behind the rear wheel, but it was enough to spin the Mustang fully around, off the track, and onto the sand on the outside of turn one. I came to rest in a cloud of dust, engine dead, facing the wrong way.

In a few seconds, I'd just thrown away eleven laps of hard work. I quickly restarted the engine and grabbed first gear, but then had to wait for about half the field to go by until I could rejoin the race. Finally, there was a gap, and the corner workers waved me away. I smoked the Mustang's rear tires furiously as I got back onto the track and began to build up to racing speed again. As my hot, sticky racing slicks were now nicely covered with a layer of sand and dirt, I knew that it would take at least another lap to clean them off. It took more. By the end of lap fifteen, the tires were biting again. Then I came past the pits, where I had the real damage confirmed from Herb's pit board. The spin had dropped me from fourth place to fifteenth.

One part of me felt like just pulling off and parking it right there. Half the race was gone, I was down in fifteenth, and the leaders must have been almost a full lap ahead. And I was mad at myself. It's never a good idea to do anything that requires a lot of skill and concentration, like driving a race car, when you're mad. On the other hand, if you can turn the anger into cold determination, it can work for you. I knew that's what I had to do—for myself and for the two guys waiting in the pits who had put everything into getting this car ready for me. I owed them. I hate quitting, and I don't much like losing, either. There were fifteen laps left. Winning was out of the question, but there might be enough time to at least put on a good show.

I had spent the first half of the race in deep concentration, being careful, plotting strategy, and trying not to make any mistakes. Now I had to take chances. I knew that I hadn't yet pushed the Mustang consistently to its limit, using maximum revs on every shift, braking deeply into every corner, getting the power on earlier, and taking cornering lines that would use up every inch of the road. I began to do all of that every lap from then on, throwing the Mustang into corners, sliding out of them with the power full on, and catching and passing anyone I could anywhere there was an opening. I was driving more on nerve and adrenaline than with my head, which was why I missed every single one of Herb's pit signals for the next fourteen laps.

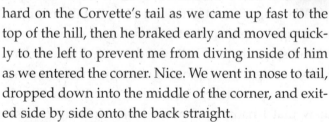

What finally woke me up was the white flag waving as I blasted past the start/finish line, which indicated that I was starting the final lap of the race. I was closing on the same white Corvette that had pushed me off earlier. This guy I had to catch, and I wanted to do it in the Corkscrew. I was hard on the Corvette's tail as we came up fast to the top of the hill, then he braked early and moved quickly to the left to prevent me from diving inside of him as we entered the corner. Nice. We went in nose to tail, dropped down into the middle of the corner, and exited side by side onto the back straight.

If I was going to get by, it would have to be in the final corner. My brain was in control again, and I lifted slightly to let him in front of me through the fast kink leading up to the final left-hand turn. Then I put

my foot down hard and darted to the inside, taking the line for the corner. To hold the inside line, I had to lock up all four wheels under braking, which started the Mustang sliding sideways as we entered the corner. I quickly grabbed second gear, steered into the skid, gave the Mustang full throttle, and exited the last corner almost sideways, with the Corvette right behind.

Payback.

The Mustang snapped straight, and then it became a drag race with the Corvette to the finish line. Both our engines screamed well past maximum on every shift, but the Mustang held its ground and took the checkered flag no more than a foot ahead of the charging white Corvette. And then the Mustang's engine let go in the biggest possible way.

Chapter 8

Impact

There was no warning, just a loud metallic bang, and the engine noise stopped instantly. Everything immediately went white, as if I was in a plane that had suddenly flown straight into a cloud. The cockpit of the car filled with thick, white smoke, stinging my eyes and nose. I couldn't even see the steering wheel, much less the road ahead. Blind and powerless, I was still moving at well over 100 miles per hour as I felt the rear end of the Mustang starting to come around. At this point I was no longer a driver, just a passenger along on an uncontrolled ride to the nearest wall. Definitely not a good feeling. I stood on the brakes and braced myself against the steering wheel, praying that I wouldn't hit whatever was out there. Or at least that it would be something soft.

The car seemed to be slowing down, but I knew that

it couldn't just keep on sliding and eventually come gently to rest. There was too little road left and too many guardrails and barriers.

Then the impact came, like a huge fist in my back.

Full stop.

Everything was suddenly, eerily, quiet and still. My first impulse should have been to get out. Instead, I sat motionless, gasping a bit to get back the wind that had been knocked out of me. But I really sat there not because of fear but out of simple respect for this car, which we had taken months to build and I had now smashed in a second. It had given all it had in the race, and now it wrecked itself protecting me. It had done everything Herb told it to. The Mustang sat— spent, crippled, and deathly silent. All of this went through my mind in a few moments, but it felt like an hour. Sitting there just seemed the right thing to do, until the acrid white smoke from the engine brought me back to my senses.

I quickly released the harness, tore back the window net, and dove out onto the ground, just as the corner marshal's truck arrived. I got up and backed a few steps away from the crumpled, smoking Mustang. The car had slammed backward into a concrete retaining wall, the impact crushing the right rear corner. A trail of engine oil lead back from the crash site for several hundred yards. I had blown the engine, spun on my own oil, and finished up hard against a concrete retaining wall. One of the marshals ran up, took my arm and walked me slowly over to their truck. She sat me down in the passenger seat.

"OK, nice and easy now," she said calmly. "That was quite a ride you just took."

She helped me unbuckle and remove my helmet and gloves, all the time moving slowly and looking at me very closely, very seriously. I smiled back weakly.

Then the questions began. "What's your name?" she asked.

"Eddie."

"What day is today?"

"Saturday."

"Where are you?"

"Laguna Seca, California."

"And where are you from?"

"Seattle. Well, Vancouver, B.C., originally."

"What's the area code for Vancouver?"

"It's 604 for B.C. I don't know for Seattle, and I'm OK. Really. My neck's a little sore, but I'm still all here." I wriggled my fingers and tapped my toes together to prove it. She relaxed a little and smiled.

"Very impressive. All the same, you've had a heavy impact. We want you go back in the ambulance to the track medical center and let the doc have a look at you."

"I'd rather stay here with my car," I protested.

"Don't worry. We'll make sure it gets back to your crew."

The ambulance had arrived and I was escorted by two paramedics into the back and quickly whisked away.

My unplanned medical checkup took about half an hour. The doctor said little but made sure that there wasn't any damage to my back and neck, and that there was no concussion. He told me I would probably have some neck and back pain for a few days, and gave me some painkillers and muscle relaxants. I thanked him and walked out of the medical building. Rick was waiting right outside the door, beaming for reasons I didn't understand right then.

"Eddie! Doc says you're OK?"

"I'm OK," I replied. "But he did tell me that my neck might be—"

"Great, Eddie, great! Herb's back at the trailer with the car. It's a mess, but we'll sort that out later. Come on! We've missed the podium presentation, but they want you over at Race Control right now."

We began walking the short distance to Race Control in the main tower. The podium presentation was for the first-, second- and third-place finishers, and I really didn't care that we had missed it. Good for those three guys. All I had done was drive flat-out to the finish and wreck the car. I felt bad about it, and I wasn't in the mood to get excited about who had been on the podium.

"Look, Rick, forget it. Let's get back to the pit. I really want to see what shape the Mustang is in. I'll check in with the officials later. I mean, it's not like I won the race or something," I said.

Rick stopped and then said thoughtfully, "You're right. You didn't win the race. That white number 5 Mustang from L.A. did. A Camaro was second."

Then he broke into a grin. "You were third."

I didn't believe it. "Third? No way. The highest I got was fourth early in the race, but then I spun and dropped back to fifteenth. You guys wrote that on the pit board. P–15. Remember?"

"Yes, I do. And I also remember a lot of other stuff that happened. I remember that you drove flat out from then on. That you broke the Trans-Am lap record. Twice. That three guys who were in the top five early on didn't even finish. And that you caught and passed that white Corvette and held him off at the finish. And you know what? Not once did you look at the pit board for the last half of the race. So, how do you know where you finished?" he demanded.

"Well, I guess I don't exactly," I admitted. I really wanted to believe him, but it still didn't add up. "Not third. Never. It couldn't have been third...could it?"

"Well, let's just go right on in and find out, shall we?" Rick replied, as he held open the door to Race Control and ushered me in.

Three race officials were sitting at a long table covered with timing sheets. A large middle-aged man stood and greeted us.

"Eddie Stewart," he announced, reading my name off my driving suit. "A very impressive performance, son!" he said, smiling broadly. "It's too bad you missed the podium presentation. You deserved to be there."

Rick elbowed me. "Told you," he whispered.

Then he shook my hand firmly and handed me a check for eleven thousand dollars.

"Congratulations on a hard-earned third place, Eddie."

A second official joined him, also shook my hand, and handed me a heavy brass-and-wood trophy. Rick was beside himself. "Yes! Yes! Third! Twenty-four cars—and we're third in our first Trans-Am!"

Rick loves to do impressions of movie stars and singers, and he's just awful at it. Elvis Presley, his favorite, is by far the worst. He went into it right then.

"Thankya. Thankya very much." He spread his arms wide and bowed to us.

The officials glanced blankly at each other while Rick started in, singing the opening bars of "Heartbreak Hotel."

"Is he always like that?" one of them asked me.

This was getting embarrassing. "Well, ah...no, not always. Just when he's really happy. Like now." I hurried Rick toward the door.

"Does he know 'Blue Suede Shoes'? I like that one," a second official asked.

He did. Rick instantly made a smooth transition to this latest request. I almost had him out the door.

"Thanks, but I'll take him home now. He needs food. Rest. Medication."

I forced a quick smile, dragged him out, and kicked the door closed behind us. As we walked back to our pit, Rick used the trophy as a microphone and crooned his way through "Blue Christmas." I was stopped twice along the way by other Trans-Am drivers who offered their congratulations. One of them was even the guy in the white Corvette that I had battled with.

Reaching the end of the pit area, we found Herb's feet, sticking out from under the Mustang. He had the car—stripped of its bodywork and wheels—up on stands and was surveying the damage. He spoke to us from under the car.

"So, Eddie, is that Rick with you, or did you find Elvis in the medical center?"

"Thankya, but it's really me, Herb," Rick answered in a deep Memphis drawl. "It's old Ricky. But I know it's kinda hard to tell."

Herb crawled out from under the Mustang, stood, and extended his hand to congratulate me. I was still a bit slow after the accident and wasn't thinking. We shook. It hurt.

"Third! All right!" Herb exclaimed. I passed him the trophy and the check with my good hand.

"Third's great, you guys, but I want all of that money to go back into fixing the Mustang," I said.

Herb read the check carefully, passed it back, and looked at me narrowly.

"Are you sure you're OK, Eddie? Doc checked you out?"

"I'm fine," I replied, nodding to the car. "So, how bad is it?"

"Well, it stood up pretty well. Took a big hit, but eleven grand should about cover it. The engine's history. Broken rod, hole through the side of the block. Might be useful as a boat anchor for your dad, though. We've got three spare engines back at the shop, so I'm not too worried."

He pointed to the rear of the car. "But *that* I might lose some sleep over."

I squatted down for my first close look. It was a real mess. Thankfully the fuel cell hadn't been damaged, and I stopped myself from thinking what might have happened if it had split open. The entire rear corner of the frame had been smashed into a ball of twisted metal tubing, right up to the rear wheels. And that was just what we could see. I knew that an impact hard enough to shorten the car by a foot would have huge damage that we had yet to find.

"Bottom line, we'll have to completely rebuild the frame from the driver's seat back—including a new rear axle, suspension, brakes, and bodywork," Herb stated.

Rick crawled under the car and offered his opinion. "Exactly right. And we'll rejig the whole chassis to make sure it's still straight. Man, you must have really hammered that wall, Eddie."

I nodded and rubbed my eyes. I was beat and the painkillers weren't even touching the dull pulses of pain from my neck. I pushed my hair back, looked at my hand, and was surprised to see that it was shaking. The physical efforts of the race and the shock of the accident were beginning to catch up with me. I stood up slowly, feeling the stiffness beginning to creep into in my back, shoulders, and arms.

"OK, here's the plan," I announced. "I'm going to get changed and cleaned up. We'll lock everything up, and then I'm taking you two out to dinner. My treat. Name the place. "

"Good deal," said Herb, as he gathered up his tools. "I know the best place in Monterey. We passed it on the way in, right on the coast."

"I know it," Rick said. "That open-air market down by the wharf. Seafood it is." He assumed that, as Monterey is right on the Pacific, we were off to wolf down plates of steaming shellfish.

Herb was shocked. "Seafood? Excuse me, gentlemen. Please. Nothing so ordinary. Tonight, we dine at Bob and Edwina's International Pancake Emporium."

Chapter 9

The Pancake King

Team dinners on the road were usually pretty basic. Sometimes it was burgers, or if we had time, a reasonable restaurant, where Rick would go for seafood and I'd stick to some pasta. Herb would order the usual three double-cheeseburgers, double fries, and a couple of milkshakes anyway. But if he could find a pancake house, we were in for some serious dining.

As soon as we'd parked, Herb was out of the truck, through the doors, and straight back to the kitchen, where he compared notes with the cooks about pancakes. Rick and I shuffled in, found a window booth, and waited. I was about ready to use our new cellphone to order a pizza and have it delivered to our table, when Herb finally slid back into the booth.

"So, is it OK to order now?" Rick said impatiently. "We're ready to eat the place mats here."

"Just had to check things out, guys," Herb said, scanning the menu. "No problem. They know what they're doing."

A cheerful middle-aged waitress arrived. "Hi, boys! I'm Helen. What can we get for you?"

"Oh, I don't know," Rick sighed. "Just buttermilk pancakes with ham and coffee, please." He was less than thrilled.

"Same for me, thanks," I said, folding and handing her my menu.

Helen smiled and waited patiently. Herb was still studying the menu with intense concentration.

Finally, he looked up. "Helen, do you recommend the blueberry pancakes, or the boysenberry at this time of year?" he asked.

To my amazement, she actually paused and thought this over.

"A difficult choice, sir. Normally I would suggest the blueberry. We have had an unusually dry spring, however. I find that the blueberries are lacking their usual firmness and that their flavor is less robust."

Herb, the blueberry expert, nodded, understanding completely.

"And the Belgian waffles?"

Helen brightened. "Ah, our Belgians are always excellent! In fact, they are our specialty, precisely prepared according to Edwina's grandmother's recipe."

I leaned over and whispered to Rick. "Who knew? Edwina's grandmother, the Waffle Queen of Belgium."

We rolled our eyes at each other. Now that we had revealed ourselves as pancake barbarians, Helen gave us an icy glare and turned her full attention to Herb.

"Sir, for someone of your obviously refined tastes, might I recommend the Belgians with our own boysenberry sauce, a dusting of powdered sugar, and a very light Vermont maple syrup?"

"That will do nicely, " Herb stated with satisfaction, snapping his menu closed. "For openers, I believe I will also try the blueberry and boysenberry pancakes as well. Even with a hint of dryness, I'm sure they will still be up to standard."

"At once, sir!" Helen announced. Clearly impressed, she spun on her heel and rushed our order immediately to the kitchen.

Rick and I stared silently at Herb across the booth for a long moment.

"What? You guys just have no appreciation for fine food."

"Herb," I replied. "Look around. We're in a pancake house. We're sitting in an orange vinyl booth at a lime-green table. We have paper place mats with pictures of baby dolphins on them. Fine food? I wanted to treat you guys to a really good meal after today."

"Yeah," Rick said. "I was looking forward to some fresh fish, poached or maybe grilled, with a big salad, fresh bread…" Rick's voice trailed away as he sighed heavily.

"Look, you guys, there's nothing wrong with pancakes or waffles," Herb replied sternly. "It's the most underrated food group in North America."

"Right up there with deep-fried donuts and a wiener on a stick," Rick replied dryly.

Herb ignored this remark and lectured us for the next five minutes on the nutritional components of pancakes, two dozen of his favorite types, exotic syrup flavors, the raging butter-versus-margarine debate, and on and on. Rick and I had heard this before, but we let him continue. It passed the time.

Helen arrived with our order ten minutes later, single plates for Rick and me, and three heaping plates for Herb. I reviewed the Mustang repairs with Rick as we ate, but Herb was totally focused on savoring every mouthful, alternately eating from each of the three plates, mixing little pools of syrup, and humming happily to himself. Often his eyes were closed.

Rick and I finished quickly, pushed our plates away, and began to sketch out some ideas for a new rear frame section design on a place mat, between the baby dolphins.

"We can move the fuel cell forward a bit in this new section, which will improve weight distribution and access to the suspension," Rick explained. "What do you think, Herb?"

"Whatever you say," Herb replied absently, as he dabbed the corners of his mouth and slid out of the booth. "Keep at it. I've got to congratulate the chefs."

Over the next half hour, Rick and I pretty much redesigned the entire rear end of the Mustang, while Herb talked shop with the cooks and Helen kept the coffee coming. When he finally came back, he was beaming and carrying a large takeout box.

"Got some extras for snacks a little later," he explained. "And just look at this!" He took several handwritten sheets of paper from his shirt pocket.

"Edwina gave me three recipes. Belgian waffles, potato pancakes, and her own blueberry syrup!"

I paid the bill, and left Helen a nice tip. We searched for and found a motel near the track, and Rick and I turned in right away. Herb stayed up to snack on his fourth order of pancakes and watch an old episode of *Star Trek* on a Mexican cable channel. I fell asleep to the aroma of cold potato pancakes and the sound of Mr. Sulu firing main phasers in Spanish.

Chapter 10

Sophie & Caroline

We got back to Laguna Seca early Sunday morning, with plans to secure the truck and trailer and then hike around the track up to the Corkscrew to take in the Formula Atlantic and Champ Car races. As we wheeled into our pit area, however, we found that access to our trailer was completely blocked by a very large and very new motor home.

"Well, isn't that nice?" Rick observed as he parked the truck.

We got out to see who had decided to camp out in the middle of our pit area. I walked around to the side of the motor home, and knocked briskly on the door. Someone pulled back a window curtain slightly, and then there was a muffled scream. Strangely, it was a scream I knew, but I couldn't immediately place it. In another moment I would have had it, but just then the door flew open. There was a second, higher squeal from inside, and then a very large woman in a brilliantly flowered housecoat burst through the doorway, grabbed me with both arms around the waist, and lifted me right off the ground. My aunt Sophie.

"Eddie!" she exclaimed, loud enough to make race teams in the pits stop and look. "And Rickie! And Herbie!" I don't know why Sophie had always added "ie" to their names. My friends and I had always been "the boys," and I guess she thought it was cute when I was five. She saw Rick, dropped me like a sack of laundry, rushed over, and gave him the same bearhug lift; then she tried it completely unsuccessfully with Herb.

Aunt Sophie was one of those people who didn't attract attention; she demanded it. In her early fifties, with mounds of curly silver hair and sparkling brown eyes, Sophia Novello stood a little over five feet tall and weighed in at a solid two hundred pounds.

Although she was almost as wide as she was tall, Sophie had energy to burn, talked constantly, wore the loudest clothes possible, and had a booming, infectious laugh. She was a great lady. After I lost Mom, she stepped right into the role. She had adopted Herb and Rick as well, and the three of us flat-out adored her.

"Aunt Sophie!" Herb grinned as he withdrew from the bear hug. "You look great."

"Of course I do! I look wonderful," Sophie agreed, "and now I feel wonderful. I have found my boys."

"Sophie, what are you doing here in Monterey?" Rick asked. "In this huge motor home? What about the restaurant in Vancouver?"

Sophie smiled slyly.

"I have sold it, Rickie. Gone! Sold it to a development company from Hong Kong—for condominiums or something. They wrote me a very big check, and I decided it was time to see America. So I bought this motor home and called your parents. They told me you boys were racing your car here this weekend, and so I am here!"

She spread her arms toward the motor home. "Gorgeous! It is like driving my living room around!"

"But when did you get a driver's license?" I asked. I'd known Sophie most of my life, and she had never driven a car, much less owned one.

"License? I do not need one, Eddie." she winked. "I have my own driver. Caroline is with me."

Caroline Grant was Rick's younger sister by a few years. They both shared their parent's blond hair, blue eyes, sharp intelligence, and bizarre sense of humor; but there the resemblance ended. Rick called her the "weird child," not because she actually was weird, or a child anymore, but just to underline to everyone how different Rick and Caroline were from each other. Rick was tall, slim, and usually logical. He believed that the world could only be understood through math and science. Caroline was of medium height, athletic, and artistic. She saw the world through art and images. Rick liked to observe and analyze while Caroline preferred to participate and create. I'd often thought that if I wasn't driving Rick's race cars, then someone like Caroline would be.

I hadn't seen her for almost three years. When we all went off to college, Caroline finished high school. Then she left to study art and photography in London, England. Rick had informed us that lately she was studying computer graphics, filmmaking, and business management, as well as painting. My last memory of Caroline was of a bright, energetic girl of seventeen, who loved adventure and always seemed to be laughing about something or someone. Usually Rick or me. I also secretly remembered that she was really cute, but I had never admitted that to anyone.

"Caroline!" bellowed Aunt Sophie. "I have found them!"

Caroline stepped gracefully through the door, smiling brightly—a little older, a little taller, and way more attractive than any of us remembered. In the presence of striking female beauty, some guys can fall all over themselves trying to be cool, clever, and charming. Not us. This was Caroline. Actually, it was a super-model who had once been Caroline. We just stood there, stunned. She crossed to Rick and hugged him.

"Big brother Richard. You look great! And a real race car guy. I'm very proud of you," she said. And it was obvious that she meant it.

"The Man of Steel!" Caroline squealed in delight as she reached up and around Herb's thick neck for a second hug. Then it was my turn.

"And Fast Eddie Stewart."

She said my name softly and, for some reason, stopped short of a hug. Instead, we just stared at each other and then sort of shook hands for a long moment. I lost my gaze in those impossibly blue eyes. I smiled crookedly. I knew that this was one of those moments. I had to impress this vision of feminine brilliance standing before me. She was waiting for me to say something. Something cool, smooth, confident, mature.

"Hey," I said vacantly.

She looked equally deep into my eyes for a moment—and then burst out laughing. It was the same explosive, infectious laugh that I remembered. She instantly had us all laughing with her and at ourselves. Or probably me, actually.

"Come on, kids! Breakfast!" Sophie announced, and she herded us into the motor home for orange juice, toast, fresh fruit, and oatmeal. I was thankful it wasn't pancakes.

After breakfast and real coffee, we left Sophie to suntan on the roof of her motor home and walked the outside of Laguna Seca track to find a good vantage point for the day's racing. We were equipped as spectators with coolers, sunscreen, and lawn chairs. Caroline packed two Nikon digital cameras with large telephoto lenses and a tiny DVD video camera, planning to shoot several disks of images. We walked for almost an hour before finding a spot just downhill from the Corkscrew, under the branches of a huge oak tree.

"Perfect!" Rick announced, setting down his cooler. "We're right next to the track, so we can see them coming out of the Corkscrew and on down the back straight." I sat down on the thin grass and stretched my back, which was still sore from yesterday's crash.

"Old age, Eddie?" Caroline quipped as she sat down and took a bottle of cold mineral water from the cooler.

"No, just lousy driving," I offered. "Yesterday I backed the Mustang into a wall a little too quickly."

"So I understand," Caroline said. "But you made the sports section this morning. Sophie read it to me before you guys arrived. They said you were the highlight of the Trans-Am race. Eighteenth to third? Broke the lap record? Doesn't sound too bad."

"We did OK, but, thanks to me, we've got a lot of work to do in the next three weeks before the race," I replied.

Rick joined us and sat down.

"OK? Well, thanks to Mr. Modest here, we're on the podium in our first pro race, and we've got eleven thousand bucks in the bank. Listen, you did what you're supposed to do, Eddie. I designed the Mustang. Herb built it. And we did that for one reason only, to see it compete with someone in the seat who can take it right to the limit. Your job is to get everything out of it that we built in. And yesterday you did. So what if you stuffed the car? We'll fix it. But we're not interested in watching our driver cruise around, play it safe, and finish eighteenth—*that* we can't fix."

I appreciated the support. Actually, I needed it. I knew that I could drive a race car, but I still hadn't been sure that I was ready to go up against professionals. Yesterday had proven some things. Herb hadn't said it out loud, but I knew that he too was pleased with my performance. For a race crew, rebuilding a top-three car was infinitely better than waxing one that would always finish near the back of the field. I relaxed, sat back, felt the sun warm my face, and waited for the field of Atlantic cars that we heard in the distance to arrive on their pace lap.

Chapter 11

Brake Test

Twenty-nine Formula Atlantic cars came toward us out of the Corkscrew, all tightly bunched up behind the brilliant red Porsche pace car. With their front and rear wings and open wheels, Atlantic cars looked exactly like smaller versions of cars run in Formula One or in the Indy 500; and their twin-cam Toyota engines snarled as they darted side to side, warming their tires. The two bright yellow Ascension Motorsports cars from Brazil, which I had seen yesterday, led the pack as the fastest qualifiers. The number 3 car was fairly plain, but his teammate in the number 4 car had bright green stars on both wings, red lightning bolts down the sides, and "Raul DaSilva" painted in huge red letters next to the driver's cockpit.

Herb pointed to the number 4 car as it passed our

vantage point. "So, you think this guy's name is Raul, maybe?"

"And don't you forget it," Rick answered.

Most drivers have their names on their cars, along with those of their crew. It was tradition. Our Mustang had my name in small script above the driver's door, and Herb and Rick had their names on the rear fenders. But I had never seen anyone as blatantly obvious about it as Mr. Raul DaSilva. Caroline was snapping a series of pictures as the field passed us. She lowered her camera and turned to me.

"Great-looking cars, but what's with this Raul guy in the yellow car? He might as well have a neon sign on his car that says, 'Hey, Look at Me! I'm a Star!'"

"No kidding," I laughed. "I guess he wants to make sure that the team managers know who he is. They don't pay much attention to the Trans-Am, but they do scout new talent in the Formula Atlantic series. They're like the triple-A teams in baseball. A step up to the big leagues. Lots of drivers in Champ Car, IndyCar, and even Formula One raced in Formula Atlantic before they moved up to the big time. This guy's looking to do the same, and if he wins today, everyone will know his name. It'll help him get noticed."

Caroline brushed back her thick blond hair and raised her sunglasses.

"Well, I think if he wants to get noticed, then he should stick to driving. Like maybe he should go out and break the lap record a few times. Something like that." She looked at me and smiled.

The Atlantic field had disappeared from view, but we could still hear them. The Trans-Am cars used a rolling start, but in Formula Atlantic, all the cars had to come to a stop on the main straight for a standing start, as in Formula One. Once they were lined up properly, the drivers spun their engines up to about nine thousand RPM, the starter dropped the green flag and they would all charge away in a wild dash for the first corner.

Even though we were a good mile from the grid, we heard the start like a wave of rolling thunder. There was an eerie quiet after they got through the first few corners, then we heard them again as the field streamed up the hill. They would be storming out of the Corkscrew in a few moments.

"Any bets on who the leader is?" asked Herb.

"Could be any of ten different guys. Atlantic is a really competitive series," I replied.

Rick sighed. "Just so long as it isn't that Raul guy. I really hate arrogance. Here we go!"

In a flash, the field burst out of the Corkscrew and accelerated hard downhill, near where we were standing. To everyone's disappointment, Raul DaSilva did in fact have the lead, but only by a few feet from his second-place teammate and three other cars that were hard on their heels. The rest of the pack followed, still tightly bunched. In less than ten seconds, all of them were past us and howling away down the back straight.

"Well, that was quick," said Caroline. "Maybe we should have watched from the stands."

"Nah. Boring," Rick replied. "On a road course you can get close to the cars where the drivers really work them hard, like here. Sit in the stands and you can see more of the track, but you're away from the action."

Herb, opening a can of soda, agreed. "Here, we're maybe thirty feet from the track. You can hear, smell, and actually feel the cars coming. Lots more fun." He glanced down at his watch. "And they'll be by again in about a minute."

Right on time, the Atlantic cars rocketed past us a second time. Incredibly, DaSilva shot past, alone in the lead now, with a gap of several seconds on his teammate. At least half a dozen cars were jammed up tight behind him—all scrambling to find a way past, and then go after Raul.

Herb whistled softly.

"Man, old Raul must have some kind of engine in his car to pull out a four-second lead on the first lap. But all those engines are built, inspected, and sealed by Toyota. So maybe—"

"So maybe he's that good," I finished Herb's sentence for him. "Or maybe he's getting some help."

Ten laps later, Raul's lead was up to over ten seconds, and we were becoming convinced that it wasn't because of his driving. Raul was quick enough all right, but his second-place teammate was lapping just fast enough to keep about six challengers behind him. And away from Raul. In frustration, one of them punched his fist out of the cockpit of his car and shook it angrily.

"How can they let him get away with driving like that?" Caroline demanded. "Can't they make him pull over?"

I shook my head.

"The marshals will show him a blue flag which means that faster cars want to pass. But it's up to them to find a way by, and it doesn't look like he's giving them any room or making any mistakes. And in an open-wheeled car, you don't want to make contact with anyone. Ever. So, unless the race officials disqualify him with a black flag for unsportsmanlike or dangerous driving, all those guys behind him will have to find a way around. Or wait."

By fifteen laps, Raul was long gone. His teammate, seeing that his work was done, then smoothly sped up to match Raul's lap times, preserving the gap and keeping himself from getting into too much trouble with the officials. To people in the stands or on TV it probably looked like DaSilva had simply used his fabulous driving skills to streak away into an early lead while the rest of the pack sorted themselves out. We thought differently. It looked like deliberate blocking. I seriously wondered if Raul and his teammate had planned and rehearsed this whole routine—and if they were better actors than racers. Rick didn't wonder. He was sure that was what they were up to, and he had been making calculations on the back of a race program that proved it.

"Something stinks here. I've been timing Raul and his buddy for the last ten laps. Raul's always been about a second and a half faster every lap. Until the last two. Just when Raul has a nice big lead. Then his teammate suddenly speeds up to match his pace."

With seventeen of the scheduled twenty laps completed, the field had become strung out around Laguna Seca. Raul had a huge lead, but he would have to pass some slower cars on his way to victory.

And it was in doing this that his race almost came undone right in front of us.

Raul came out of the Corkscrew right on the tail of a slower car—the red triangle on its rear wing indicating that it was being driven by a rookie in his first race. The rookie purposely went to the wide side of the track to let DaSilva through, but in his impatience, Raul had already moved his car there. Thinking he was being blocked, Raul slashed across to the inside, pulled in front to cut the other car off, and then quickly stabbed and released his brakes for an instant with his left foot, while still accelerating with his right. This move was known as a "brake test," and it was designed to terrify the guy behind you into locking up his brakes while you were still on the gas and pulling away. It was a dangerous move in any sort of car, especially cars with open wheels.

In an instant, the rookie's right front wheel touched Raul's left rear, which launched the front of the rookie's car a good five feet into the air. Raul's car twitched briefly from the contact, then sped away. The rookie wasn't as fortunate. His car slammed down hard, out of control, and spun wildly off the track directly toward our vantage point. We had maybe a second to step back and duck before it thumped into the guardrail right in front of us with a dull thud, followed by a shower of dirt, broken red fiberglass, and other debris.

It was a solid impact. We sprang to the guardrail, looked down, and saw the crumpled, steaming Swift Atlantic car, the driver motionless, his head slumped forward. The sharp smell of raw fuel filled the air. The smart thing to do at that point would have been to step well back and wait for the corner marshals to arrive. And maybe we would have, if Caroline hadn't dropped her cameras and vaulted right over the guardrail.

"Caroline!" I yelled.

She ignored me and went straight to the car, while I leapt over the guardrail after her, with Herb and Rick close behind. The engine had stopped, but the electrical system was still functioning, powering the fuel pump, which was spraying gas from a severed fuel line all over the back of the car as well as onto the driver. And near the engine compartment. There were a lot of very hot parts in there that could easily ignite the fuel and flash the car into a fireball. Every second counted.

"Eddie, shut off the master electric switch!" Herb yelled. "Look for it on the roll bar! Rick, find that fuel leak! Caroline—"

"I'll support his head," she replied, turning her face

away from the spray of gasoline that had already soaked her arms and back.

Herb and Rick pulled away what remained of the shattered fiberglass bodywork, and quickly traced the leak to a torn fuel line hanging loose under the rear suspension. Herb grabbed the line and folded it in half to cut the fuel flow, while I found the master switch, killing the power to the pump.

A moment later, the driver came to, snapped his head up, and immediately began complaining of severe pain in his feet. There didn't appear to be any neck or upper-body injury, but there was always the chance. While all of us wanted to get him out as quickly as possible, the best thing to do was to try and keep him still until professional help arrived. All the same, if there had been a fire, I would have immediately grabbed the shoulders of his driving suit and pulled him out. No driver would leave another in a burning car.

In less than a minute, four marshals arrived on foot. One of them took over for us; the second doused the rear of car with white powder from a fire extinguisher; and the others waved double yellow flags and redirected race traffic around the accident site. One of the marshals, a small, bald man, glanced at the three of us.

"Ambulance is on the way. You guys are either really brave or really stupid to have jumped the fence like that."

"It's OK," Caroline replied confidently. "These three are racers. They know what to do. And I'm an artist. So, no problem!"

The ambulance arrived quickly, and the paramedics carefully pulled the driver out. It was clear from the pain he was in, and from the grisly outward angle of his right foot, that this rookie's season was over. They brought a stretcher over, gently lifted the injured driver onto it, and whisked him off to the medical center. With all the activity from the accident, the race organizers had put the whole track under a full-course yellow-flag condition. This meant that all the cars had to slow right down and stay in single file behind the leader. With only two laps left, there wasn't enough time for the crash scene to be cleaned up and to allow racing speeds to resume.

All of which meant that the race finished under the yellow caution flag in a slow single-file procession. Headed by Raul DaSilva, coasting home to victory.

Chapter 12

The Raul DaSilva Show

We climbed back over the guardrail as a tow truck pulled up and hooked a steel cable under the roll bar of the wrecked Atlantic car. The gasoline was stinging and starting to eat away at our skin, so Herb dumped some ice water from a cooler to wash our hands and arms. But Caroline's back and neck were looking worse by the minute. One of the marshals called to us.

"Hey! You guys are going to need to get that fuel washed off. And the head race steward will want to talk to you about this accident. Some of the other teams are complaining about the number 3 and 4 cars. There's going to be at least an hour's delay, so jump in and we'll give you a lift back to Race Control."

We would have preferred to keep our spot to watch the Champ Car race, but that was becoming painfully impossible. And we did have eyewitness information that the race officials might need. We threw our gear in the back of the truck, and rode back to the pits with the marshals.

As soon as they dropped us off, Herb took Caroline straight to Sophie's motor home to shower. Rick and I washed up in the driver's locker room, and then went to Race Control to talk with the stewards. Their job was to oversee the entire organization of the race weekend, including investigations of accidents and protests from other drivers. After the Atlantic race we had just seen, they were going to be busy.

We stepped into the small office in the control tower. One official was on the phone, while the other two, their backs to us, were reading over yellow protest forms. I walked over to the desk.

"Hi. We saw the accident in the Atlantic race and helped get the driver out. The marshals thought you might want to talk to us."

The chief race steward turned and rose from behind the table. He was the same large man with the slow southern accent who had presented me with my third-place check yesterday. He smiled slowly.

"Well, I thought you just were a hotshot Trans-Am driver, son. Now you're a daredevil spectator?"

I returned the smile. "Not really. It happened right

in front of us. The driver was out cold, fuel spraying everywhere. So I followed my—"

"Zing!" Rick interrupted. "Eddie went right over the guardrail in one leap! He was chasing his girl-friend."

"Really. Chasing your girlfriend?" asked the puzzled race steward.

"No!" I protested. "I was just—"

"Actually she's my younger sister," Rick stated helpfully. "But she's Eddie's girlfriend, all right. Except he doesn't know it. Neither does Caroline, probably. At least not yet. Anyway, it doesn't really matter, because they've always kind of had this thing for each other, you know what I mean? Even when we were growing up back in Van—"

I snapped my right hand hard over Rick's mouth and kept it there. I took a couple of deep breaths, then spoke slowly and evenly.

"Please excuse my motormouth friend here. First, I do not have a girlfriend. And even if I did, I don't know that I'd be chasing her over guardrails. Second, Caroline and I are just good friends. That's all. We're not, like, well, you know…"

"I'm not exactly sure I *do* know," said the steward, with a sly smile.

"We are…but we're kind of not…I think…. Look,

I'm just here to discuss the crash. Period."

I lowered my hand from Rick's mouth and raised my right index finger to him in silent warning. He smiled, rolled his eyes, and shrugged. One of the other race officials leaned over to his boss and whispered something while looking suspiciously at Rick. I caught the words "Elvis" and "medication."

The head steward sighed and nodded. "Well, I'm sure that your romantic life must be real interesting, son. And I know that your friend here may not be...let's just say that he might not be firing on all cylinders."

He winked at me. Rick was ready to protest the comment, but I warned him with a cold, menacing glare.

"Just tell us what you saw."

Rick began. "OK. We watched the whole race just downhill from the Corkscrew. Raul what's-his-face took off and built a huge lead while his teammate held everybody else up. On purpose, I think. I timed the gaps. So, Raul runs off and hides until near the end, when he comes up to lap this poor rookie who crashed. The rookie gives Raul lots of room on the inside. But as soon as he passes the rookie, Raul cuts in and brake tests the guy."

The stewards looked at each other hard when they

heard the term "brake test." They knew what it meant and how dangerous that move could be.

"So," I continued, "The rookie's car climbs the back of Raul's rear wheel, gets launched, comes down hard, and spins off—straight into the guardrail right in front of us. The nearest marshal station was at the top of the Corkscrew, so we jumped the fence and helped. The rest, you know."

The chief steward took a sip of coffee from a Styrofoam cup, collected his thoughts for a few moments, and made some notes on a form.

"So, your view of all this is that Raul DaSilva caused the accident? Not the inexperience of Mr....here he is—Mr. Bill Baker?" he asked, checking the Atlantic entry list.

"I know Baker's a rookie and that he's going to make mistakes," I said. "But from where I stood, I'm sure that he saw Raul coming, and moved over. There was no reason for DaSilva to cut him off and nail the brakes other than anger at being held up for a second or two. Baker did the right thing. DaSilva didn't," I said evenly.

The steward looked at Rick. "You see it the same way?"

"Absolutely," Rick stated.

"Well, I'll add your opinions to the rest. And we are

going to be having a word with Mr. DaSilva." He placed his notes onto a pile of half a dozen other protest forms. "Thanks for coming in."

We turned to leave.

"And Eddie—" I was surprised that he remembered my name.

"This business is about winning, and some guys think it's OK to win at any cost. Part of my job is to make sure they don't get to do that. To see that they win clean and within the rules. And after the race you drove yesterday, that's part of your job now, too. It's part of being a professional. Don't feel bad about coming forward. You did the right thing."

We left quietly and walked down the hallway, just in time to catch Raul DaSilva in the middle of a loud interview with a television crew. Out of his race car, DaSilva was short and slim with jet black hair, dark, fiery eyes, and sharp features like a hawk. Judging by his rapid chattering and quick hand gestures, he was pretty worked up.

"I am two laps from victory, and this idiot tries to block me! Me! The leader! And when I am forced to get around another way, what does he do? Bang! He hits me in the back! I am almost punted from the road!" he exclaimed.

Raul was backed up by about half a dozen of his

millionaire friends, and his performance had drawn a small crowd. Rick and I stopped and joined it.

"And now, I am told that I must report here and explain my actions to some official! Me—Raul DaSilva, Formula Three champion of Brazil, the man who dominated and won the race today—I must explain my driving? What of this fool who hit me? Where is this man?" he asked, looking around the crowd. No one had an answer. Except Rick.

"He's in the hospital with a crushed foot. He's done for the season," Rick stated.

Raul looked over at us and nodded, a thin, cold smile playing across his lips.

"As he should be. Unfortunate, but such is the cost of foolishness. The man had no business competing with seasoned profession- als."

Usually, I'm able to let comments like that slide. But Raul said it with such cold, pure arrogance and conceit, and with such callousness, that I couldn't let it go.

"So then, I suppose he should have expected you to pass him, and then cut across his nose and jump on the brakes?" I asked loudly, looking right at

Raul. "Is that what seasoned professionals do?"

Raul returned my hard glare for a few intense moments, trying to work out what to say—to decide whether he should admit to anything or not. Finally, he looked away and said to the reporter, "That did not happen. He is mistaken." Then he spun and walked quickly past us to the race steward's office with his fan club in tow.

The television crew shut down, and we left Race Control and began the long walk back to Sophie's motor home to meet up with Herb and Caroline. On the way we came upon Bill Baker's pit and his crunched Atlantic car.

Rick stopped for a closer look. "You know," he said,

walking slowly around the car, "other than the footbox, front suspension, undertray, and some body damage, it's not that bad. Definitely fixable."

Two men in pit uniforms came out of their trailer. Baker's crew.

"You're right," said the taller of the two. "We could have it ready in a week or so. But our driver's out for two months, probably three. Wish I'd seen what happened."

"Your guy touched wheels with the leader and got airborne," I said. "He came down, lost it, and nailed the guardrail. The front end of the car took the worst of it. Fuel line got sheared off, but it got sealed, and the electrics were shut off before anything ignited."

They looked at us in surprise. "How could you guys know all that?"

"Because we were there," Rick replied. "At the crash site, downhill from the Corkscrew. We jumped the fence and shut things off. Good thing, too, because your driver was unconscious, with fuel spraying all over everything."

The crewmen looked at each other. "So, you were the guys who rescued Bill! The marshals mentioned something about that to us. He's still at the track clinic, but I'm sure he would want to thank you. And so do we."

We introduced ourselves, and Rick invited them to stop by Sophie's motor home later. Rick was unusually quiet and smiling to himself as we walked back to the motor home.

He was up to something.

Chapter 13

A New Road

Caroline was drying her hair with a thick white towel as we stepped into the motor home. Herb's rendition of a TV game show theme was coming through the bathroom door, and Sophie was happily chopping vegetables for one of the three pots she had simmering on the stove. There was a strange but not unpleasant odor of shampoo, pasta sauce, and gasoline.

"About time you two got back," Caroline said. "Herb's in the shower. That gas sure made a mess of my skin. Look at my arm." She pulled up her sleeve to reveal several large red and inflamed patches.

"Ouch," I observed. "Only one thing worse than that," I whispered, just loud enough to ensure that Rick would overhear.

"Worse? Like what?" she asked, tossing the towel aside and reaching for a hairbrush.

I glanced over at Rick, who was busily hunting through the cupboards for snacks. It was a perfect opportunity for some payback.

"Well, I heard about a guy just the other day—and I'm not making this up—who actually drank it," I said.

Caroline was wide-eyed. "No way! Drank racing gas? Imagine what that would do to your insides. What a lame stunt. You'd have to be totally stunned!" she exclaimed.

I nodded slowly and seriously, watching Rick out of the corner of my eye.

"No kidding. You would have to be totally stunned. In fact, this same guy—"

Rick saw where I was going with this and jumped in quickly. "Tragic story, Eddie. Really tragic. Hey, look! I found some cookies. Here, put five or six in your mouth. Well, it looks like we're all cleaned up, so come on, let's get back out. Time to watch the Champ Cars. Time's wasting."

"And what is the rush, Rickie?" Aunt Sophie asked,

as she joined us. "Herbie is still in the shower." She crossed the kitchen and banged on the door loudly. "And no one has had lunch!"

We all knew better than to argue with Sophie when she was in the mood to cook. Which was about every two hours. We could hear the Champ Car engines warming up, but it didn't matter. Lunch was being prepared. And we would be eating it no matter what. Sophie hummed happily and began to prepare pasta salad. Herb emerged dripping from the shower, was scolded and lashed with a tea towel for soaking the floor, and then told to grind beans for real coffee. Rick, Caroline, and I set the table in the dining area.

There was a knock at the door.

I opened it to see a balding, middle-aged man in a wheelchair, wearing shorts and a golf shirt, with his right leg in a cast. I looked up and recognized the two crewmen standing beside him. It was the unfortunate Mr. Baker, ex–Formula Atlantic driver.

"Hi. I'm looking for Eddie and Rick," he stated.

"I'm Eddie. Rick's inside," I replied. "We'd invite you to come in, but I don't think you'd fit."

"It's OK," he said. "I'm afraid this cast is going to keep me out of tight places for a while. I'm Bill Baker. I heard about what you and your friends did for me after my accident, and I really wanted to thank you guys. Could we talk out here?"

"Sure," I replied. I called the others to join us, and we set up some folding chairs and a table next to the motor home. Delighted to have company, Aunt Sophie brought out three extra plates. Rick passed around some cold cans of soda, and we all sat down and made short work of the pasta salad. Despite his broken leg, Bill Baker thoroughly enjoyed it and asked for seconds. His crew men complimented Sophie on her recipe. She beamed. Then Baker sat back carefully in his wheelchair, wincing as he tried to find a comfortable position.

"Well, this is a day to remember," he said. "First, you four pull me out of a wreck. Maybe saved my life. And then I have some of the best Italian food I've enjoyed in years. I'm a lucky man."

He raised his can of soda. "A toast. To bravery and pasta."

We all clinked cans and drank to that. Herb drained his in four gulps and was ready to crack another when Sophie and Caroline froze him with an icy stare. Baker smiled thinly.

"My crew tells me that my car isn't too bad, but this leg is going to be in plaster for the rest of the season. I was really looking forward to getting some pro experience this year."

"We just had our first pro race yesterday," Rick said proudly. "We have a Trans-Am Mustang. Number 75. Finished third!"

"And stuffed it into the wall," I said quietly under my breath.

"And broke the lap record. Twice," added Caroline, beaming.

Baker leaned forward, interested. "I watched that race." He looked over at me. "You were driving that red Mustang?" I nodded.

"That was some drive! What happened to the car?"

I explained how the engine blew and how I had spun in my own oil, hitting the wall and crushing the back end of the Mustang.

"We've got a lot of work to do in the next three weeks, but we'll be ready," Herb stated.

Rick had removed his glasses and started to clean them quickly, his brow furrowed in thought. This was rarely a good thing. Rick always did this when he was processing lots of information, working out alternatives, and planning strategy. He was in turbo-brain mode, and I had no idea why. It always made me nervous.

Rick replaced his glasses and looked up. "Mr. Baker, you also have some work to do on your Atlantic car, although quite a bit less than our Mustang. Anyway, even if your car is repaired, you still won't have the most important ingredient."

He was floating an idea.

Baker was listening intently. "What would that be?"

"That would be…," Rick smiled broadly, "a racing driver. And we just might happen to have one available."

All eyes turned to me. Herb had been quiet up to now, but he joined the conversation with energy.

"Fast Eddie here won the Pacific West amateur Formula Ford and GT1 titles in the last two years. He lies awake at night, dreaming about Atlantic cars. Don't you, Eddie?"

"I don't lie awake dreaming, Herb," I replied.

Rick couldn't resist this opening and whispered loudly to Sophie, "Unless it's about the young and lovely Caroline."

Sophie giggled quietly. I was about to kick him in the shin, but Caroline beat me to it with a solid slug to her brother's shoulder that nearly rocked him out of his chair.

I continued. "Dreaming aside, yes, I would love a shot at an Atlantic car. All of us would, someday."

Rubbing his shoulder, Rick went on, "So, Mr. Baker, Herb and I can design and build just about anything. Our Trans-Am car proved that yesterday. What are your plans? Are you just going to park that car until next year? Or do you want to see it run?"

Baker saw where this was going. He shifted position again before replying.

"Well, boys, I'm afraid that I'm not going to do either one. I have a wife, four kids, and a growing construction business to look after. I realized today that's where my attention should be, not out here trying to race with guys half my age. So the car will be put up for sale. I'm hanging it up," he said.

Baker's crewmen, who must have known already, quietly sipped their sodas. Caroline leaned forward with the same focused expression as her brother.

"Mr. Baker, who exactly would be interested in buying your car? Who is your target market?"

"Target market? Well, other racers. The car's brand new; just got it from the Swift factory last month. And I bought lots of the latest spare parts. This was its first race. In the right hands, it's a very competitive package."

Caroline nodded in agreement. "And how many hard-core racers are likely to read an ad in the local newspaper and come around to your garage to see this car?"

"Well, not many, I guess," Baker admitted. "It's not like anyone could take it out for a test drive."

"Exactly. To sell your car, don't you need to get it in front of the very people who would be interested in buying it?"

"That would be the best plan, but I'm not hauling it all the way to the next race in Milwaukee, Wisconsin, in a few weeks," Baker stated firmly.

Caroline smiled, winked at Rick, and played her last card. "No, you wouldn't want to do that. But we would."

I shot a glance at Herb, but he just shrugged and appeared to be as puzzled as I was. Who was "we"? Rick however, knew where his sister was going.

"Mr. Baker," he said carefully, "Here is our proposal. We have four weeks until the next Trans-Am race. That is more than enough time for our team to repair your car and enter it in the next Atlantic race at Milwaukee, with Eddie behind the wheel and a big For Sale sign on the side. You get the car out in front of potential buyers. And we will get a shot at Formula Atlantic."

Baker thought this over for a few long moments. "I see. I don't like to mention it but, well, what if you guys just disappear with my car?"

Now it was Aunt Sophie's turn.

"Mr. Baker. I am godmother to Caroline, and I have known these three boys since they were...well, since they were much smaller boys. They are all fine young men. Did they not pull you from a smoking wreck this morning? Surely they have earned your trust."

"That's true. But, what if you crash it? I mean, then it's worthless," Baker protested.

Rick replied, "So, we'll take out insurance for one race. It's expensive, but—"

"Eddie won't crash it," Herb interrupted. "Will you, Eddie?"

No pressure here, I thought. Part of me really wanted this deal to come together. But at the same time I knew we had to make a decision between fixing the Mustang and putting all our energies—and a fair chunk of our prize money—into a one-shot deal with a Formula Atlantic car we didn't even own. At best, I figured that we would get in a single race, and then have only a few weeks and a lot less money left to rebuild the Mustang for the next Trans-Am race.

"Look, I can't promise that I won't damage your car, Mr. Baker. It's a race car, and if you want to attract any serious buyers, it'll have to be a fast one. So I wouldn't be going 2,000 miles east to Milwaukee just to cruise around. I might crunch it. You would have to assume some risk. Second, I just can't support putting a bunch of our own money into a car we don't own, for one race. We've already got one car to rebuild.

And an Atlantic car is a lot more complicated than a Mustang. Where would we find the time?"

I looked at Rick and Herb. "Look, I'm sorry, guys, but I just don't think it can work."

Aunt Sophie stood, glanced at her watch, and put on a gigantic straw sun hat decorated with wax replicas of every type of tropical fruit known to man.

"Mr. Baker needs time to rest from his injuries. And to consider our proposal."

Our proposal? I must have missed the part where our race team suddenly grew from three to five. Aunt Sophie walked behind Baker and began to push his wheelchair away from the motor home.

"We'll be back in a while, kids! Have some more pasta!"

And with that, Sophie briskly wheeled a surprised and speechless Bill Baker away, with his crewmen following in her wake. Things were moving fast and Sophie was in control.

No one knew it right then, but that brief meeting was the first step on a new road for us all. Sophie was setting a course for our team that would shortly lead us directly into the seat of a Formula Atlantic car. And put us head-to-head on the track with Mr. Raul DaSilva.

We were on our way up.

Caution period. A point when the race is slowed to allow the track to be cleared.

Champ Car. A formula race car competing in the Champ Car World Series.

Data acquisition. A computer system that collects information on race car performance.

Downforce. The load placed on a car by air flow over its front and rear WINGS.

Formula Atlantic. A single-seat, open-wheeled race car.

Gearbox. Contains gears that the driver shifts to transmit engine power to the wheels.

Grid. The starting lineup of cars, which is based upon qualifying times.

Marshals. Race track safety workers.

Oversteer. When the rear wheels lose their grip and a race car slides or spins.

Pace lap. A slow warm-up lap before starting the race.

Pace car. The official car that leads the race car field during the pace lap or caution period.

Paddock. The area where teams park transporters or set up garages.

Pit. The area where teams work on the race cars.

Pit board. A sign that is held up by the pit crew to inform their driver of place, race position, and lap.

Push. Another term for UNDERSTEER.

Podium. A stage where the top three race finishers receive their awards.

Pole position. The first starting position, which is awarded to the fastest qualifier.

Qualifying. Timed laps that determine where each car will be positioned at the start of the race.

Rain tires. Deeply grooved, soft compound tires that are designed for racing in the rain.

Setup. Adjustments that are made to the race car by crew members.

Slicks. Treadless racing tires.

Suspension. A system of springs, shocks, and levers that are attached to the wheels and support the race car.

Trans-Am. The Trans American Championship for modified sports cars

Understeer. When the front wheels lose their grip and the race car continues straight rather than turning.

Wets. Another term for RAIN TIRES.

Wings. Direct airflow that passes over the race car, pushing it down onto the track.

ANTHONY HAMPSHIRE is as comfortable strapped into the seat of a race car as he is in front of a classroom. Raised in London, England, and Calgary, Alberta, Anthony has been a racing driver and team manager, a football coach, and a magazine columnist. He was also a classroom teacher and educational technology consultant and is now a school principal. Anthony has earned national and provincial awards for his work in school curriculum and media, authored educational software, and is a regular conference presenter and workshop leader. He makes his home at the foot of the Rocky Mountains in Alberta, where he lives with his wife, two daughters, and a bossy Welsh Corgi.